YOU ARE A GREAT AND POWERFUL WIZARD

AN OVERVIEW OF HUMAN MAGIC AND SPELL CASTING

THE ORDER OF RADICAL CATS

1st Edition

First Edition, November, 2016

Published in the United States by the Rad Cat Press.
Designed by Sage Liskey.

Printed in the United States of America
1st Edition

ISBN 9780986246128

www.sageliskey.com
www.facebook.com/radcatpress
radcatpress@riseup.net

$\mathscr{T}$ABLE $\mathscr{O}$f $\mathscr{C}$ONTENTS

$\mathcal{I}$NTRODUCTION

YOU ARE A GREAT AND POWERFUL WIZARD

Every word spoken, thought made, motion moved, and energy exchanged is a magic spell conjuring up a new set of possibilities that changes the shape of reality. There are billions of spells being cast each moment, but most people never learn how to control this inherent power. As a human wizard you have a great potential to become stronger by learning how to control the spells you cast and how to counter or block spells from other wizards.

*****

Note that the magic contained herein primarily influences the emotional qualities of humans, but physical changes may follow. This magic may also be used on non-human quarries.

$\mathcal{M}$AGIC $\mathcal{S}$PELLS:

Magic spells are cast through words, movements, thoughts, and energy. Once cast, spells may result in various forms of creation, destruction, neutrality, or a mixture of all three. The following are just a few of the many outcomes of a successful (or unsuccessful) magic spell:

EMPATHY	ANXIETY
LIFE	DEATH
FEAR	CONFUSION
HEALING	HATRED
CREATIVITY	INTELLIGENCE
DESPAIR	ANGER
COMPASSION	LOVE
ART	INSPIRATION
MIND CONTROL	LEARNING
SPIRIT	PASSION
COURAGE	RESILIENCE
TRUST	STRENGTH
PEACE	DISCORD

Weaving Spells Together

Life is complicated. It cannot be controlled by a single word or motion. Some spell effects may only be obtained by weaving together many different types of spells.

For instance, in order to successfully cast a LOVE spell, one must cast the spells of PASSION, TRUST, COURAGE, EMPATHY, and possibly others. LOVE takes time to cast and is difficult to control even for adept wizards utilizing ideal conditions.

Counter Spells

Don't let unwanted magic get to you, cast plenty of defensive barriers and learn a few counter spells for when destructive magic is flung your way. Remember that destructive spells can come from outside of or from within you. The best defense for either source is a strong mind able to remain aware and prevent unnecessary thinking. Ready your arsenal with spells that evoke:

LOVE
EMPATHY
COMPASSION
GRATITUDE
HUMOR
PATIENCE
TRUST

GROUP SPELLS

A group of entities may gather together to collectively cast magic. If done properly, a group spell will be much stronger than an individually cast spell. These may take the form of:

RITUAL
CELEBRATION
COMMUNITY
MEDITATION
POTLUCKS
FRIENDSHIP
LOVE

Controlling Your Magic

Some spells are harder to control than others. These spells require a lot of training to cast properly and may need to be periodically recast to work effectively.

- *Speak with conviction by using motion and emotion.*
- *Think in the present moment without stressing about the past or future.*
- *Speak the language of the one whom your are communicating with.*
- *There are many ways to cast the same spell.*
- *There are many ways to create the same spell effects.*
- *Some magic will only work in the right time and place.*
- *Your spell effects are especially influenced by the greater pool of magic being cast by other wizards.*
- *Magic that is negative or destructive to the user often casts without your awareness. Be careful.*

$\mathcal{P}$OWERING $\mathcal{U}$P

YOUR LANGUAGE

- *Practice the language you are casting a spell in.*
- *Take communication courses.*
- *Learn Nonviolent Communication.*
- *Take language courses and learn new languages.*
- *Speak to many different types of people.*
- *Understand different communication styles and cultural dialects.*
- *Use dictionaries and thesauruses.*
- *Travel and visit other nations.*
- *Study etymology, sociology, and psychology.*
- *Understand the needs of the person you are trying to cast a spell on or block a spell from.*
- *Learn the true meaning of a word through life experiences and engaging in a wide variety of activities.*
- *Understand the communication nuances between extroverted, introverted, and shy wizards.*
- *Sing and become a musician.*
- *Write poetry.*

$\mathcal{P}$OWERING $\mathcal{U}$P

YOUR MIND AND THOUGHTS

- *Meditate. Speak with the great void of nothingness and find great powers by quieting your mind.*
- *Say positive mantras to overwrite negative thought spells.*
- *Build your creativity by solving problems and making art.*
- *Learn coping methods for when stress arises.*
- *Address forms of stress (see the final page for resources).*
- *Work for something beyond yourself.*
- *Engage in a world free of rules, restrictions, and money. Be willing to be yourself.*
- *Break down your cultural, societal, and gender norms.*
- *Join a community that helps you power up your mind.*
- *Free yourself of unhealthy habits.*
- *Deconstruct your belief in good and bad.*
- *Understand that life is death and death is life.*
- *Free yourself of desire.*
- *Explore the dream realm.*
- *Maintain a gratitude journal.*

$\mathcal{P}$OWERING $\mathcal{U}$P

YOUR BODY MOTIONS

- *Exercise and work out.*
- *Stretch.*
- *Practice facial gestures in the mirror.*
- *Dance.*
- *Let go of your fear of being silly.*
- *Dress in a way that allows for freedom of motion and makes you feel good about yourself.*
- *Utilize clothing that enhances your motion-based spells. For instance, clothing with tassels or flowing folds.*
- *Practice acting.*
- *Learn the accepted body motions of the wizards in your area.*

$\mathcal{P}$OWERING $\mathcal{U}$P

YOUR ENERGY

- *Address your sources of suffering (see the final page for resources).*
- *Learn how your body uniquely regulates energy.*
- *Understand how different foods and substances influence your body's energy.*
- *Visualize your energy by learning about major and minor chakras.*
- *Learn how to control your emotions.*
- *Express your emotions freely.*
- *Engage in group spells that improve your energy.*
- *Meditate.*
- *Explore the subconscious mind through your dreams and become a lucid dreamer.*
- *Dismantle your concepts around duality and of good and bad.*
- *Join a spiritually based group and become spiritually grounded.*
- *Befriend your soul and unlock your powerful soulular potential.*
- *Become in tune with nature's cycles of light, weather, astral movements, and color.*

Magic Potions

Sometimes you need a little help casting a magic spell. If used properly magic potions may temporarily or permanently enhance your magical abilities. Misuse of magic potions may also lead to ill effects or an untimely demise. Tread with caution!

HEALTHY FOOD
CLEAN WATER
CLEAN AIR
MEDICINES
ADAPTOGENS
VARIOUS HERBS

$\mathcal{W}$IZARD $\mathcal{W}$ANDS

Various objects may be used to strengthen the magical powers of a wizard. These wands come with their own unique set of characteristics that when used properly amplify the effectiveness of your spells. Try these wands for powering up:

MUSICAL INSTRUMENTS
MIRRORS
CLOTHING
TRINKETS THAT GIVE YOU STRENGTH AND JOY
THE INTERNET
SOCIAL MEDIA
COLOR
MAKEUP
THE MOON
THE SUN AND STARS
FIRE
PERFUME
NATURE
LIGHT
DARK
YOUR BODY
ART

Imbuing Objects
With Magical Power

You can imbue any object with magical power by concentrating your magic into it. Imbued items may be used as a source of ENERGY, LOVE, POWER, ANGER, FEAR, JOY, and so on. Imbuing objects with "positive" magic is most easily accomplished using gifts received from other wizards or creatures of the earth, as that entity has already imbued some positive energy into the item. You can also use items that various wizard cultures have collectively imbued with magic such as flowers, feathers, and rocks. Be warned that "negative" and destructive magic will strongly attach to any object without warning. Train in your wizardly practices to avoid these magical misfires.

People need a key in order to unlock the magic power trapped within an imbued object. If you are gifting a magically imbued item to another, tell them how to access the item's power.

Examples Of

Common Spells

* I LOVE YOU * I HATE YOU * YOU'RE AMAZ-
ING * YOU'RE AWFUL * I BELIEVE IN YOU * I
DON'T BELIEVE IN YOU * THANK YOU * MAY
YOUR DAY SHINE LIKE THE SUN *

* I'M AFRAID * THERE'S NO POINT IN TRYING *
TODAY IS A BRAND NEW DAY WITH GREAT
POTENTIAL * I'M NOT GOOD ENOUGH * I'M
BEAUTIFUL *

* A SMILE * A HUG * A KISS * AN EXCITED
JUMP * A FROWN * A SNICKER * A GLARE *
LAUGHTER * A GIFT *

* CLEARING YOUR MIND OF ALL THOUGHTS *
CLEARING YOUR MIND OF ALL JUDGEMENT *
PRAYING FOR SOMEONE * ASKING FOR
FORGIVENESS * EMBODYING A SENSE OF
REVENGE AND HATRED * EMBODYING A
SENSE OF JOY AND LOVE * NAMING
AN OBJECT *

$\mathscr{P}$ARTING $\mathscr{W}$ORDS

There is one final thing to say before we conclude our overview of wizardly magic. All destruction leads to creation and all creation leads to destruction. Furthermore, there is no definitive "good" or "bad" magic, only the will of the wizard or group of wizards casting a spell. A powerful wizard knows how to use magic in order to achieve destruction or creation that is beneficial to their personal wizardly ambitions.

Now that you know your true power as a wizard, The Order of Radical Cats wishes you well on your grand journey through time and space.

And always remember,

YOU ARE A GREAT AND
POWERFUL WIZARD

Magic Notes

$\mathcal{R}$AD $\mathcal{C}$AT $\mathcal{P}$RESS

The Rad Cat Press is devoted to the distribution of life-changing and accessible information. We invite you to read our other works which may aid in your wizardly adventures. You can find us on Facebook at www.facebook.com/radcat-press or visit www.sageliskey.com to peruse our projects and free downloads:

~THE HAPPIEST CHOICE: ESSENTIAL TOOLS FOR
EVERYONE'S BRAIN FEELINGS~
~THE HAPPIEST CHOICE: CONDENSED EDITION~
~A CENTURY OF MOON PHASES~
~WINE AND POETRY NIGHT YEAR ONE~
~A SUSTAINABILITY GUIDE FOR EVERYDAY FOLK~
~COMMUNITY HOW TO~
~SURVIVING THE COLLAPSE OF SOCIETY:
SKILLS TO KNOW AND CAREERS TO PURSUE~
~THE TRUTHAGANDIST PRIMER: EFFECTIVE
INFORMATION DISTRIBUTION FOR ACTIVISTS~
~THAT WAS ZEN, THIS IS SUDOKU!~

CPSIA information can be obtained
at www.ICGtesting.com
Printed in the USA
BVHW081509120921
616490BV00002B/220